MAX E. JAMES

BOOKS 1-3

AN EARLY READER CHAPTER SERIES

J. RYAN HERSEY

Illustrated by Gustavo Mazali

TABLE OF CONTENTS

FIRST FREE DOWNLOAD

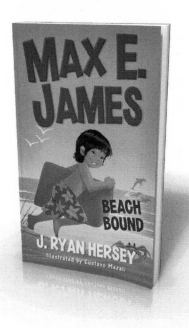

**What adventures await Max
during his trip to the beach?**

Get your free electronic copy of the first book
in the Max E. James children's series.
Type the link below into your browser to get started.
http://www.maxejames.com/books/beach-bound/

SECOND FREE DOWNLOAD

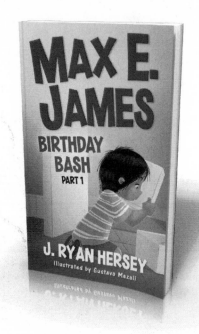

Will Max's one and only birthday wish come true?
Join my Kids' Club to get your free electronic copy of the second book in the Max E. James children's series.Type the link below into your browser to get started.

http://eepurl.com/cfcfkj

MAX E. JAMES
BEACH BOUND

J. RYAN HERSEY

Illustrated by Gustavo Mazali

MAX E. JAMES

BEACH BOUND

J. RYAN HERSEY

Illustrated by Gustavo Mazali

This is a work of fiction. All names, characters, places, and situations are the product of the author's imagination. Any resemblance to actual persons, living or dead, events, or locales is coincidental. No part of this publication may be reproduced, or transmitted in any form or by any means, electronic or otherwise, without written permission from the author.

To my family – the source of my inspiration.

CHAPTER 1

Waiting

"OH MAN," I said. "Trapped in my room. Again." It was pitch black except for the glowing red light from my desk. The numbers on the clock read five-four-three.

How could I, Max E. James, be stuck in my room? One of my parents' rules, that's how. The rule says I can't come out until the first number on the clock reads six. Thanks, Mom and Dad.

I stared at my clock for what seemed like an hour, but the numbers didn't change. Must be broken.

"That's it," I said. "Rules don't count if the clock's broken."

I grabbed Fuzzy, my best attack blanket, and tip-toed to my bedroom door for a peek down the hall. No sign of life from my big brother Cody's room. Hmm, it was a little too quiet. I remembered that Cody told me once that monsters hide in dark silent halls. Fuzzy eats monsters.

"Go get 'em!" I shouted, launching Fuzzy into the hall.

I slammed the door shut, pressed my back against it, and counted slowly.

"One...two...three...four...five," I said. "That should just about do it. Any monsters left, Fuzzy?"

I cracked the door. No trace of any beasts.

"I can always count on you," I said. "I hope they tasted good."

I grabbed Fuzzy and crept into the living room to watch cartoons.

"Would you look at that?! The clock on the TV says five-four-three, too!" I exclaimed. "What are the chances?"

I wrapped Fuzzy around me and left a small peeky hole for just my face. I felt the couch bounce as I flipped through the channels. It was Cody. He plopped down next to me and before I got a word out, he snatched the remote.

"Hey, no fair," I said. "My turn to pick."

He glared at me and turned back to the TV. I didn't stand a chance.

"That's what I thought," he said. He yanked Fuzzy away and bundled him around his feet!

"Gross," I said. "Get your dirty piggies off my blanket!"

Cody just smiled and dug his toes in deeper. I clenched my teeth, reached for the closest pillow, and swung it at his big fat head.

Faah-whap! The force sent him sailing off the couch onto the floor. The remote crashed down beside him.

"Serves you right," I said.

"You'll pay for that," he said, wobbling to his feet.

I slid off the couch and backed away.

"Ahhh! Mom-my!" I cried. "He's going to get me!"

I raced towards my room and heard a thud behind me. What was that? I turned around and slammed into Daddy, then fell backwards onto the floor. When I looked up, I saw that he was wearing a frown.

"Oh. Hello, Daddy," I said. "It's still early. What are you doing up?"

"What's going on, Max?" he asked. "It sounds like a herd of elephants out here."

"No pachyderms," I said. "It's just—"

"He hit me in the face!" Cody said. "And made me fall, too."

"No, I didn't," I said. "It's not my fault you can't walk."

"Is everybody okay?" Daddy asked.

"Yup," I said.

"I guess so, but my butt hurts," Cody said.

Daddy knelt down, rubbing his forehead. "Let me see."

Cody pointed to a red blotch just below his hip.

"Mommy said not to rub your head like that,"

I said. "Remember? It will give you a retreating hairline."

Just then, Mommy walked out of their room, giggling.

"Good morning, gentlemen," she said. "By the way, Max, that's a *receding* hairline. But you're right, Daddy's hair is retreating." She kissed us each on the cheek and walked down the hall.

"Oh, and, Daddy," she said, "it's only 5:50. Should they be out of their rooms this early?"

Daddy smiled at Cody and me. He leaned close. "You boys know the rules. Back to your rooms."

So there I was, right where I started. Trapped. The worst part? I didn't even find out what we were going to do today. I looked at my clock. It said five-five-one.

CHAPTER 2

Mommy's Pearly Whites

"THANK YOU, SIX." I said. "I'm free at last." I ran to the kitchen and was greeted by the smell of bacon and pancakes. My favorite!

"Well, good morning, again," Mommy said. "Please wash your hands before you sit down."

"What?" I said. "But I haven't even touched anything dirty today. They're clean, see?"

I stretched my hands into the air and wiggled my fingers inches from her face.

"Go wash your hands," Mommy said, laughing.

I washed them as fast as I could and was back to the table in a flash.

"Yummy," I said. "I love the smell of bacon."

"And the taste, too," Cody said.

My first bite was almost spoiled by a horrible smell: Daddy's coffee.

"Yuck, Daddy," I said. "Your liquid stink is ruining my taste adventure."

He must have choked on that nasty stuff because he spit some out all over the table. Coffee must taste as bad as it smells.

I leaned close to him and smiled. He smiled back. Now's my chance! I jammed my fingers into his mouth and yanked on his two front teeth.

"Ouch!" he said. "What in the world are you doing?"

"Well, you drink coffee."

"Uh-huh."

"So I wanted to see how easily your teeth came out. They're really stuck in there good."

"What are you talking about, Max?" Mommy asked.

Cody stopped chewing and stared at me.

"What?" I said. "I saw it on TV. Old people take their teeth out to clean off coffee stains. They put them in cups of bubbly water."

Cody rolled his eyes. "Those are dentures, genius. You know, fake teeth."

"Oh, I forgot," I said. "You're nine now so you know everything."

"Dentures are for really old people who don't have their real teeth anymore," Cody said. "You have to be like thirty or forty to get them."

Unfortunately, the roar of laughter from Mommy and Daddy saved Cody from getting in trouble for making fun of me.

"One thing's for sure," Daddy said. "That boy is getting too much screen time."

Cody looked up at Mommy's bright red face. "How old are you?"

"I'm thirty-nine, Cody," Mommy said.

"Oh," he said.

Now Mr. Smarty-pants didn't know if their teeth were real or not.

Mommy revealed all of her pearly whites with a warm smile. "Don't worry. All my teeth are real. And so are Daddy's."

We finished breakfast and I ran to my room. A t-shirt and my favorite swimming trunks had been laid out on my bed.

"Mom-my! Are we going swimming?"

"We're going to the beach, Max," she said. "But not quite yet. I still have to take a shower."

My face crumbled. "But I already had to wait once today. I can't wait anymore."

"Well, you're going to have to," Mommy said.

"Ugh," I mumbled. Time stands still when mommies are in the bathroom.

"Why don't you go help load the truck?" she said. "I think your Daddy and Cody are already outside."

As I stepped onto the driveway, the sun warmed my cheeks.

"Grab those bodyboards, Max," Daddy said.

I felt uneasy as I reached for the boards, but I couldn't put my finger on why. Their salty smell snapped me out of my trance. Oh well, I thought, and handed them to Daddy.

After everything was packed, Cody and I hopped in the back seat and buckled up.

Daddy stood outside the truck shaking his head. As he opened the door, he said, "Gentlemen, it's not time to go yet. Out of the truck."

"Can't we just wait in here?" Cody asked.

"We're so excited," I said.

"Fine, but crack the windows so you can breathe."

Cody and I smiled at each other and rolled the windows down.

"And no fighting!" He pointed his finger at us and ducked into the house.

"Yeah," Cody said. He flicked my ear. "No fighting, Max. Stay on your side!"

"Ouch!" I said. "Keep it up and we won't even make it out of the driveway."

I laid a towel across the back seat to separate our sides.

"There," I said. "Don't you dare cross it."

CHAPTER 3

Sand in My Toes

KNOCK-KNOCK. THE RAP on the window startled me.

"You're both still breathing," Mommy said as she got into the truck. "No blood even. I'm impressed."

Daddy sat down in the driver's seat and we were off.

"What do you want to do now?" I asked. "Car rides are boring."

"I don't know," Cody said. "How about a thumb wrestling tournament?"

"Sounds good to me. No cheating though, okay?"

He smiled and we interlocked hands to kick off the first match.

"One-two-three-four!" we chanted. "I declare a thumb war."

Even though Cody's older, we're pretty evenly matched when it comes to thumb wrestling. I won the first bout, then he won the second. By the time we turned onto the beach road, the score was tied at seven to seven.

"Look!" I said. "I see water."

"We're almost there," Cody said. "Last match."

He looked me dead in the eye. "This one is for all the glory."

I lunged at his thumb, but it slipped out from under my grip. That's when he extended his pointer finger and snagged my thumb. I was down for the count.

"One. Two. Three! Please welcome the all-time reigning thumb-wrestling champion of the world!" shouted Cody.

"Hey," I said. "You cheated! The Japanese Snake Attack is illegal."

"Too bad, little brother," he said. "There's always next time."

The truck ground to a halt and he wiggled his finger in my face and hissed like a snake. "We're at the beach now anyway. The tournament is over."

We cleared the parking lot and hit the sand. Cody and I sped off with our bodyboards. Mommy

followed with the towels and her purse. Daddy car-
ried everything else.

Cody and I ran onto the trail past the sign at the
base of the dunes. It said: No Walking on Dunes.

Thanks to my run-in with the park ranger last
summer, I know that the sign means no climbing
either. Or jumping and rolling. I suggested they
needed a bigger sign listing all the rules. Apparently

there is some kind of nature living there, but all I've ever seen is grass and weeds.

"Do you hear that, Max?" Cody asked.

I stopped to listen.

"Is that the waves?" I asked.

"Oh man. If you can hear them from here, they're going to be huge!"

Cody zoomed down the path out of sight.

My stomach twisted and turned as memories of last summer flooded my mind. Oh, right! I know why the bodyboards made me feel funny. The last time I bodyboarded, I face-planted in the sand after a huge wave spit me up on the beach. It was horrible! I sure hope it doesn't happen again!

Since Cody had ditched me, I walked the rest of the way with Mommy and Daddy. As we were setting up I remembered the one thing I can't stand about the beach.

"I hate sunscreen!" I yelled. "It makes the sand stick to me and Daddy gets it in my eyes. It burns."

"Well, it's either that or spend the day in the truck," Daddy said. "Your choice."

"Wait a minute."

I rummaged through the sand toys and pulled out a pair of goggles.

"There," I said, adjusting the strap and sliding them over my head. "Ready."

Daddy chuckled and rubbed the sticky goo all over me.

"Sorry, buddy," he said. "You know I have to."

Cody grabbed his bodyboard and headed to the water after Mommy finished with his sunscreen. Something caught my eye as he sprinted past.

There's only one type of nature that moves like that, I thought.

"Hurry up, Daddy," I said. "Before it escapes!"

"Before what escapes?" he asked.

"That nature over there. It's the best kind— alive!"

CHAPTER 4

Unsuspecting Nature

"COME ON, DADDY," I said. "This is taking forever."

"All done," he said.

I grabbed my net and took off. When I got to the spot where I'd seen the movement, I dropped down and crept across the warm sand. Bad move. I was instantly coated from head to toe. Human sand paper once again. Thanks a lot, Daddy.

I crawled over a mound and removed my goggles. Inches from my nose lay a perfectly round hole the size of my fist. Jack pot! It was a ghost crab lair. I peered down the dark the tunnel.

"Anyone home?" I whispered.

Nothing. There was no way I was going to stick my hand in there. I learned that lesson the hard way last summer! Instead, I jammed the net handle down the hole and it disappeared beneath the sand.

"How about now?" I said.

I wiggled the handle in circles, causing a partial tunnel collapse.

"I guess I'll have to wait you out," I said.

"Hey!" a voice called from behind me. "What are you doing?"

"Shhhhh, I found a ghost crab," I said. "He's down this hole. I'm going to catch him."

"Here, let me help you," Cody said. "He won't come if you're too close."

I shrugged my shoulders.

"You have to move farther back."

"But my net is too short. How will I reach?"

"We could build a trap!" Cody said.

"How?"

"Like you see in the cartoons. All we need is a bucket, some string, and a stick. Works every time, guaranteed."

"I don't have any string," I said.

"Go ask Mommy and Daddy. I'll keep watch while you're gone."

I took off through the sand. Turns out Daddy had some old fishing line at the bottom of the beach bag. That line would work just fine for our trap.

"Thanks," I said.

I grabbed Cody's net and stuffed the fishing line in the bucket. Now I just needed a stick.

I searched the beach but didn't even find a twig.

"Hmm," I said, wondering what else could work. "I know. I've got it!"

I pulled an old army man from the toy bag.

"Duty calls," I said and ran back to find Cody still standing guard. I dropped the supplies on the ground in front of him.

"Looks like you got everything but the stick, Max."

"I couldn't find one," I said. "Anyway, this is better."

I held the old army man close to his face.

"Meet Sergeant Crab Trap."

"What's he for?" Cody asked.

"His mission is to hold up the bucket! Sergeant Crab Trap reporting for duty, Sir!" I said in my best army man voice.

Cody smiled. "Interesting idea."

I put the bucket down beside the tunnel and waited while Cody tied the fishing line around the sergeant.

"Here you go," Cody said, and he threw it to me.

I stuck Sergeant Crab Trap in the sand next to the hole. I leaned the bucket against his shoulder, making sure to keep his view clear.

"Careful with the fishing line," I said.

Cody gently laid it across the sand. "Now, we wait."

We huddled behind a mound of sand, but didn't have to wait long before we saw something more. I tightened my grip on the line.

"Look," I said. "There it is!"

A single leg emerged. Then there were two legs but they vanished in a white flash.

"Did you see that?" I said.

"Yup. Won't be long—,"

"Look!"

Two beady black eyes popped out of the hole. They were followed by legs and a claw. He was almost completely out.

"Get ready," I said. "Just a little farther."

We held our breath in silence. My sweaty hands grasped the line even tighter.

The white crab surfaced and cautiously searched the area.

"He doesn't look so fast," I said.

"Trust me," said Cody. "He's like lightning. Pull on three?"

I nodded.

"One. Two. Three!"

I yanked the line as hard as I could. Sergeant Crab Trap skipped across the beach and the bucket clipped the crab as it fell. It scurried across the sand towards us.

"Hey," I said. "It missed. The trap is a dud."

"Have faith, little brother," Cody said.

He pointed at the bucket. It came to rest directly over the tunnel.

"We got him now!" he said. "Get him."

The crab darted across the beach frantically searching for a place to hide. Cody lunged in front of him and I snuck around behind.

"Net him, Max."

We both swiped our nets, but he scampered away. Cody threw his net as the crab ran past. He missed, but the stunned crab paused just long enough for me to scoop him up from behind.

"Yes!" I cried. "I got him."

"All right," Cody said. "I knew we could do it."

I held the net up and admired our catch. He was the size of my fist.

"Get the bucket, Max! Before he escapes."

We ran back to our stuff and grabbed the bucket. Cody filled it halfway with sand and dumped the crab in.

"Look, Mommy," I said, running toward her. "We caught a ghost crab."

It circled the bucket, trying to jump out, but the walls were too high.

"I think I will name him Hobart," I said.

"Very nice, gentlemen," Mommy said. "Please

don't leave him in there all day. He's happier when he's free."

Mommy pulled down her glasses so we could see her eyes. "Okay?"

"You mean we can't keep him?" I said. "He's our pet."

"No, Max. He has to go back to the wild before we leave."

"Okay," I said. "Whew! All that work made me sweaty. It's dripping all down my face."

"Time to get back in the water," Cody said.

He turned and raced to the ocean. I ran after him, but paused at Mommy's feet.

"Don't let him escape."

"I'll keep an eye on him," she said. "But if he gets out, I'm not touching him."

Chapter 5

Cannonball Wave

I CHASED AFTER Cody only to grind to a halt steps later. A drop of sweaty sunscreen trickled into my eyes.

"Ow! It burns!" I yelled.

Rubbing it just spread the liquid fire. I stumbled to the water's edge in a blind daze. If only I could rinse it out. I bent down and splashed some water on my face.

"Ahh!"

The salt water burned even more. I blinked uncontrollably and collapsed in misery. Tears filled my eyes. Drop by drop, they flushed the pain away.

My vision was blurry, but I could just make out a figure in the water: Cody.

"Wait for me," I said.

I waded carefully into the water as Cody dove

29

into a wave up ahead. My toes dug into the sand with each light step. Careful now. I didn't want to land on any sharp or pinchy nature. Cut feet end the day real quick.

Just then, I stepped on something soft and slippery. It was slimy and wiggled under my foot.

"Gross," I said. "Co-dy. I stepped on a big...a big, booger! And it's moving."

It flipped and flopped real mad. I lifted my foot and just like that, it was gone. At least it didn't pinch me.

I swam all the way to Cody without my feet touching the bottom. I clutched his waist and lifted my feet to his face.

"Do you see any slime?" I wiggled my toes. "Any booger pieces?"

"Are you all right?" Cody asked.

I nodded my head, so Cody pried me off and I dropped into the water.

"Don't worry. It was probably just a flounder. They lie flat on the bottom."

"Oh," I said. "Do they bite?"

"No, but they're weird. Their eyes are only on one side of their head."

"Who's eyes?" asked Daddy.

He sloshed through the water towards us.

"The flounder Max just stepped on," Cody said.

"Oh," Daddy said. "I bet that was freaky. What are you guys doing out here?"

"Getting ready for our favorite beach game," Cody said. "That is if you say yes."

"What?" Daddy said.

"Cannonball wave!" we shouted.

"Aren't you guys getting a little too big to stand on my shoulders?"

"Nope," Cody said.

"Me neither," I said.

Daddy rubbed his shoulders and stretched his arms.

"Okay, but no diving."

"Me first," I said. I swam over and scurried up his back.

"Easy now," Daddy said as I climbed onto his shoulders.

"Jump already!" Cody said.

I leapt and the oncoming wave swallowed me with a splash.

"Nice one," Daddy said. "The waves are perfect today, huh boys?"

Cody climbed onto Daddy's shoulders as I swam back towards them.

"Sure are," Cody said. "It's going to be great for bodyboarding."

"Yeah," I said softly. "But not right now, okay? More cannonballs."

We took turns jumping into the oncoming waves. As I scaled him for what must have been the fifteenth time, something caught my eye.

"What's that?" I asked.

Daddy and Cody turned to look. I pointed to the little splashes peppering the top of the water.

"Probably little fish," Daddy said. "Why do you suppose they're jumping?"

"To breathe?" I said.

"No," Cody said. "They're lunch for something bigger."

"Cody's right," Daddy said. "Fish breathe underwater. Something is definitely chasing them."

"Look!" Cody said. "Behind you!"

I turned in time to see a large dark fin slice through the water only feet from us.

Chapter 6

Digging Like a Ghost Crab

I SCRAMBLED UP Daddy's back and clung to his neck with white knuckles.

"What was that?!" I asked, frantic.

"Neck. Loosen," he croaked.

I eased my death grip.

"Look over there," Cody said. He pointed at three gray fins that disappeared in a swirl of baitfish.

"Those look like shark fins," I said softly.

"I bet they're dolphin," said Cody.

"That's a pod of dolphin," Daddy said. "Must be lunchtime. We sure are lucky to see them up close in the wild."

"Yay," I said. "Unsuspecting wild nature."

Every time one surfaced, I felt an urge to swim

with them. I closed my eyes and imagined gliding through the water holding onto a fin. Now's my only chance, I thought.

I sprang off Daddy's shoulders and paddled furiously towards the pod of dolphin. I was almost within reach when I felt a tug on my foot. I kicked and tried to jerk free, but it was no use. I gave up the struggle and turned to find Daddy holding my foot.

"Excuse me," I said. "I can't reach the dolphin with you holding me. Please let go."

"Exactly," Daddy said. "They're wild animals eating lunch. We should keep our distance."

"But I want to swim with them and teach them tricks," I said. "Does anyone have a hoop?"

"I think it's time for a break from the water," Daddy said. "Let's go play on the beach."

"But I want to stay here," I said.

"Come on, Max," he said. "We can dig a hole."

"A deep one?"

"We'll see."

We all sloshed through the water back to shore where Mommy was sunbathing.

"Looked like fun out there," she said. "Did you see the dolphin?"

"Sure did," I said. "I was going to train them, but Daddy wouldn't let me."

"Didn't even come close," Cody said. "I'm going skim boarding." He grabbed his board and was off.

I rummaged through the bag of sand toys and pulled out two shovels.

"This one's for you," I said. I motioned for Daddy to take the shovel.

Mommy giggled.

"A father's work is never done," she said.

"Okay, Max. I'll help, but I'm not going to dig it for you."

"Let's make it deep."

"Oh no," Mommy said, "No bottomless pit this time. Someone almost fell into one of your holes last summer, remember?"

"Yes," I said. "And I would have caught that man too. But you had to go and warn him."

Mommy slowly rubbed the sides of her head and glared at Daddy.

"Reasonable depth, Daddy."

I frowned at him. Just great. A reasonable depth is like those mini chocolate bars, never enough.

"Sure thing," Daddy said.

He winked at me and I smiled back, because he's just a big kid that looks like an adult. I bet he likes digging holes more than I do. It goes much faster when he helps, too. He does most of the work while I watch. He thinks I'm going to make a good manager someday— whatever that means.

"Try that," he said.

I jumped into the hole. "Not deep enough yet." I climbed out of the hole and waited patiently for him to finish.

"How about now?"

I jumped in and started scooping out buckets of sand.

"I think that's reasonable," he said. "I don't want to get in trouble with Mom."

I slid down the side and disappeared into the cool sand. I popped my head up and peeked over the edge. Daddy laughed.

"You remind me of a ghost crab," he said.

"Ghost crab?" I said. I'd forgotten all about my new pet. "Hobart! I'm coming!"

I scrambled out of the hole and raced to Mommy.

When I looked into the bucket where I'd left Hobart, all I saw was sand. "Mommy, where's Hobart?" I asked. "Didn't you watch him?"

She sat up from sunbathing and took off her sunglasses. "He's not in the bucket?" she asked. "I'm sorry, Honey. He must have escaped."

"I wonder how he got out."

I studied the bucket. There weren't any tracks or tunnels. The sand was totally smooth.

"He must have jumped out," I said and stuffed my hand deep into the bucketful of sand where he'd been.

CHAPTER 7

Hobart's Revenge

I ROOTED AROUND and discovered something hard under the cool sand. "What's that?" I didn't remember putting a rock in there. Could it be? The hard thing wiggled and I froze.

Snap!

"Ahh!" I jerked my hand out and there was Hobart, dangling from my throbbing finger. The sharp pain surged up my arm.

"Let go!" I said and whipped my hand back and forth. The crab sailed through the air and skipped across the beach. He settled a few feet from me and wobbled about.

"Bad Hobart." I shook my tender finger at him. "Pets aren't supposed to pinch."

The ghost crab retreated through the sand and

was quickly out of sight. He didn't even look sorry for what he'd done.

I turned to my parents.

"Can you believe it?" I said. "He pinched me!"

I shoved my finger close to their faces.

"See," I said. "Right there." I pointed to the broken skin at the tip.

Mommy let out a snort and covered her mouth.

Daddy turned away. I think he was trying to avoid looking at me.

"Are you kidding? This is serious! I almost lost a finger," I said, stepping closer. "And you think it's funny?"

Daddy erupted with laughter. Mommy managed to contain all but a few soft giggles.

"I'm sorry, Max," she said. "What did you expect? Are you okay?"

"I'm all right, but Hobart had to leave on account of his bad attitude."

"I guess he turned out not to be such a good pet?" she said.

"No, he wasn't." I turned back in the direction he'd fled, then felt my stomach grumble.

"Was that you?" she asked.

"I haven't eaten since breakfast," I said. "I think I need a snack."

"It is about time for lunch," Mommy said. "Cody! Time to eat."

Cody ran up, spotted the empty bucket, and shook his head.

"It was an accident," I said. "He pinched me."

"How?"

"I thought he escaped, so I dug him up."

Cody laughed. "Serves you right. You know ghost crabs burrow in the sand."

"Yeah," I said. "But I didn't think my very own pet would pinch me."

"Okay," Mommy said. "Sit down and I'll pass out the peanut butter and jelly sandwiches. We also have watermelon and chips. Please don't get sand in your food—crunchy sandwiches are gross."

"But I like crunchy peanut butter," Cody said.

Mommy squinted sharply at us, so we stopped giggling and ate.

I devoured my watermelon. It was cool and sweet in the hot summer sun.

I crunched my chips and bit into my sandwich. That's when I remembered another one of my parents' favorite rules: no swimming after you eat. They make you wait fifteen minutes before getting back in the water after eating. I kicked Cody and he looked up at me.

"Tricked again," I said.

"What are you talking about?" he asked.

"We have to wait fifteen whole minutes before we get back in the water!"

I stood and chucked the rest of my sandwich down the beach. Mommy did not miss this little act.

"Pick it up!" she snapped.

I slouched slowly towards the crust of bread.

Keow! Keow! Keow!

"What was tha—"

A lone seagull dove past my head as it swooped in and snatched up the sandy treat.

I turned back to Cody who was sprinting towards me.

"Try a chip next," he said.

"No, Max," Daddy said. "Don't throw anything."

I grabbed a handful of chips and tossed them in

the air. In an instant, a cloud of seagulls was upon us. They inhaled the offering and hovered just out of reach, hoping for more.

"One at a time now," I said. "I'm almost out."

Cody and I took turns throwing chips. The seagulls squawked and competed as they dive-bombed the crumbs.

Daddy took a step toward us. I could see his red face glistening in the sun.

"Let them be," Mommy said. She grasped his arm. "You've already warned them."

"Warned us?" Cody said. "What are they talking about?"

Splat!

I closed my eyes and felt sick to my stomach. The warm goo slid down my shoulder onto my arm. The chips I had just eaten soured in my belly. I swallowed hard against the knot in my throat.

"Eww!" Cody said. "Direct hit."

I opened my eyes to see the white sludge and gagged.

"Get it off!"

"I'm not touching that," he said and slinked backwards, but not far enough to escape his own poop shower.

Splat!

A large dropping landed right on Cody's foot.

"Yuck!" he said, kicking hard to fling most of it off.

We dropped the rest of our food and ran to Mommy and Daddy.

I expected a lecture, but they burst into laughter at the sight of us.

"Don't look at me," Daddy said between chuckles. Go wash off in the water."

"Maybe next time you'll listen to us," Mommy said.

Cody and I ran to the shore to wash off the poop.

"Use some sand to scrub so you don't have to touch it," Cody said. It seemed to do the trick.

Daddy appeared behind us in the surf. "Thirty-minute warning, boys. We have to leave soon, so it's now or never if we're going to go bodyboarding."

Before I could utter a word, he was towing us out into the waves. Suddenly, I wondered what had happened to the fifteen-minute rule.

CHAPTER 8

Time to Come Clean

DADDY TRUDGED THROUGH the water. The boards slapped the waves after he hauled us over each whitecap. Somehow we managed to hang on.

"Whew," I said. "We sure are a long way from shore."

"Okay," Daddy said. "Let me know when you see a good one."

I wiped the hair from my eyes and stared at the horizon. The butterflies in my stomach seemed to keep time with the swell.

"Be sure to paddle when I push," he said. "Soon you'll be doing this on your own."

"I want to go first!" Cody said.

"Fine with me," I said. "I think I'll just wait a bit. You know, for the perfect wave."

"I see one," Cody said. He pointed behind us. "Quick, turn me around."

"Hang tight here, Max," Daddy said.

I bobbed over the steep wave and watched him guide Cody into position.

"Now paddle," he said.

Cody thrashed though the water as the surf swept him away.

I looked up at Daddy and tried to swallow.

"Did he make it?"

Daddy shrugged his shoulders and smiled.

I heard a faint call from the beach.

"Ya-hoo!"

It was Cody. He had washed up on shore and was still on the bodyboard!

"Okay, Max. You're next."

"I'm not ready yet," I said. "Can we wait a few minutes?"

"Sure, buddy," he said. "Is something wrong?"

"No, just looking for a bigger wave," I said.

A flash of heat rushed through my body and settled in my rosy cheeks. What I really wanted was a tiny wave, and deep down I knew it.

"Are you sure you want to do this, Max?"

"Well, the truth is I've been scared ever since last summer."

"I see," he said.

Cody paddled up with a huge grin on his face. "That was awesome. I want to go again!"

Daddy smiled at me. "See, it was awesome."

"Let him take the next one then," I said. "I'm still waiting for the perfect wave."

Daddy shoved Cody onto another wave while I floated like a nervous cork waiting to finish our chat. How could I get out of this without being crunched by a wave?

"Okay," he said. "Learning something new is hard and you have to work at it. Failing can hurt, but that's how we learn."

He leaned down and put both hands on my shoulders. "You can only succeed after you fail. Got it?"

"Yeah," I said. "I get that waves can cram sand in all your cracks and crevices even with a bathing suit on."

"That's true," he said. "But it's normal to crash."

"My feet went over my head, Daddy. I had to pick sand out of my teeth for days. You call that normal?"

"No. But that wasn't a normal wipeout. You'll do better today."

I looked down at the water and shuffled my feet in the sand.

"You can swim, right?"

I nodded.

"Can hold your breath?"

"Yeah, I guess."

"Didn't we spend almost an hour jumping into breaking waves?"

"Uh-huh."

"How's that any different?"

"For starters," I said, "my face didn't get pounded into the sand. Which hurts."

"Does it hurt enough to make you not want to do this?"

"Not do what?" Cody asked as he paddled up. "Catch a wave?"

"I want to do it, but I'm scared," I said.

"There's nothing to be afraid of," Cody said. "Wiping out doesn't hurt."

I shook my head and stepped backwards.

"Easy for you to say. You don't wipeout."

"Anymore," Cody added. "I don't wipeout, any-more. When I was your age, I crashed all the time. That's how I learned."

"You did?" I said. This was news to me. It never

occurred to me that he wasn't born a good bodyboarder.

"Sure," Cody said. "But I always got back up and tried again. If everyone thought like you're thinking now, nobody would walk."

"Huh?" I said.

"How many times do you think babies fall before they get it right?"

I thought for a minute and felt a surge of courage rise within me.

"I think I'm ready now."

Cody winked at me and turned back towards the ocean.

"Great, Max," Daddy said. "Let's go catch one."

All of a sudden, Cody paddled furiously past us. "Must...get...over...it."

I turned back to see a wall of water rolling towards us.

Cody gave me a thumbs-up. "You can do it, Max." Then he drifted out of sight.

"Too late to escape it," Daddy said. "Hold on tight."

He spun me into position and gave me a shove. I felt the power as I rose from the sea. Time stopped and all was quiet in the shadow of the wave. My only thought was that I was glad no one could see the warm trail of courage leaking from my swimming trunks.

CHAPTER 9

Head Over Heels

I CLUTCHED THE board tight to my chest. My fingernails dug into the foam as I shut my eyes and sped down the steep wave. I was still gaining speed when I heard what sounded like a clap of thunder. It was the wave breaking! I knew I had to hold on a little longer. And just like that, the board slowed and my knees dug into the sand. I opened my eyes to find I had washed up on the beach and was surrounded by bubbly foam.

"I did it!" I said.

Mommy applauded from behind me. I stood in the knee-deep water and bowed to Daddy and Cody in the distance.

"How fun was that?" Mommy said.

"It was awesome. I can't wait to go again."

"I knew you could do it, Max."

"Thanks."

Cody washed up behind me and put his arm around me.

"That was a gnarly wave," he said. "You're crazy."

My chest swelled with pride and my smile stretched from ear to ear.

"Let's go again," I said and took off through the waves.

"Hey guys," Mommy said. "This is your twenty minute warning. I'll start packing while you catch a few more waves."

We ran until the water reached our waists and paddled the rest of the way out.

"We're on the clock, Daddy," Cody said pointing to the beach. "Mommy's packing up."

"Let's not waste any time then," he said. "Come on."

We spent the next twenty minutes riding wave after wave. I turned to catch another and noticed Mommy pointing to her wrist. I tapped Daddy on the shoulder and pointed.

"I'd better go help her," Daddy said. "You think you can manage the last wave without me?"

We nodded. I guess you're never too old to get in trouble with Mommy, and Daddy knew it.

"Don't worry," Cody said. "I'll help Max."

Daddy smiled and turned towards shore.

Cody and I glided over a few small waves. He bobbed beside me, holding my board close to his so I didn't slide out of reach. Luckily, we didn't have to wait long.

"That one looks good," he said and shoved me into its path.

"Wait!" I said. But it was too late. The wave scooped me up and I was headed for shore.

It didn't feel right. I rose up too fast and it

crested too soon. I started down the wave and felt the back of the board lift. The next thing I knew, I was gasping for air and tumbling toward the shore. The salt water burned as it shot up my nose. I eventually escaped from its foamy grasp and dragged my bodyboard onto the sand.

I was standing at the water's edge coughing when I felt a friendly hand on the back of my neck. It was Cody.

"Are you all right? That looked pretty nasty."

"It was," I said and spit out some sand. "But I'm okay."

Cody rubbed my sandy hair.

"Let's go before we have to walk home."

We rinsed off and changed into dry clothes before getting into the truck. I felt a cool burst of air as I opened the door. The air conditioning felt wonderful.

"I bet you boys are tired," Mommy said.

"Not hardly," I said.

"Me either," Cody said. "I want to stay longer."

"Well I am," Daddy said. He closed the door and sank into the seat. "Everyone buckled up?"

We nodded.

"Let's go," Mommy said. "Hey boys, what was your favorite part of the day?"

"Bodyboarding," Cody said. "No wait, catching Hobart. Hmm. I don't know."

"Bodyboarding, even though I was scared at first," I said and turned to Cody. "Thanks for the help."

"What are big brothers for?" Cody said.

I slumped into my seat and relaxed. But the blowing air conditioning made my eyes start to sting. I adjusted the vent and rubbed them. Must be irritated from the saltwater. I'll just rest them for a minute.

Clank!

I opened my eyes and glanced down at my shirt. There was a small puddle of drool. I wiped my chin as my door opened.

"I guess you were tired after all?" Mommy said. "You slept all the way home."

"I only closed my eyes for a minute. Wow! Time travel."

"I don't know about that," she said, "but time passes quickly when you sleep."

I scratched my chin and grinned. "That is good information."

Cody and I made our way into the house, collapsed onto the couch, and flipped on the television.

"You guys relax while we get cleaned up and ready for dinner," Daddy said.

"Dinner?" I said. "Is the day almost over?"

"I'm afraid so."

"Thank goodness for that!" I said.

Daddy looked puzzled and took a step closer. "What? Didn't you have a good time today?"

"Of course I did," I said. "How could you ask a question like that?"

"I guess I just expected a little more resistance. I didn't think you'd be happy about the day ending."

I looked at him real funny.

"Are you feeling okay?" he asked.

"Daddy," I said. "Come closer."

He leaned in. "Yes?"

"You probably don't know this, but I discovered time travel today.

"I see," he said.

"It only works when you sleep," I said. "So the sooner I get to bed, the faster I'll wake up."

"And then what?"

I smiled. "Then I can find out what we're going to do tomorrow!"

MAX E. JAMES

BIRTHDAY BASH

PART 1

J. RYAN HERSEY

Illustrated by Gustavo Mazali

MAX E. JAMES

BIRTHDAY BASH
PART 1

J. RYAN HERSEY
Illustrated by Gustavo Mazali

Failed

To my beautiful wife, Claire – the only person I know who can tie a water balloon as fast as I can.

Chapter 1

An Early Surprise

IT WAS STILL too dark to get out of bed. Even my big brother Cody wasn't awake yet.

"Ugh," I whined into my pillow. I pushed down the covers and stared at the ceiling.

How could I, Max E. James, not sleep? Today is my birthday and we're having a party! I've waited a whole year already and only have a few more hours to go. But hours feel like days when you're as excited as I am.

I closed my eyes and tapped my fingers on the headboard. At least it was quiet so I could figure out how to make my birthday wish come true. Last year, it was apparently delivered to the wrong James address— a mistake I won't repeat.

Ring-Ring. Ring-Ring.

I bolted upright in bed. My heart pounded in

my chest. Was that the phone or my imagination? Who could possibly be calling this early?

Ring-Ring. Ring-Ring.

This time I was sure I heard it. I sprang from my bed and burst into the hall. Monsters lurking in the hall weren't as scary as a grumpy family on my birthday. I shut my eyes, held up my blanket, Fuzzy, and tore down the hall to the kitchen.

Ring-Ring. Ring-Ring.

I fumbled for the phone in the darkness.

"Hello," I whispered.

"Max?" a soft voice said. "It's me, Jo-Jo."

"Hello, Jo-Jo," I said. "Are you allowed out of your room this early?"

"Not really," he said. "But I couldn't sleep."

"Me neither."

"Also, I wanted to be the first to wish you happy birthday. You're seven! Happy birthday!"

"Gee, thanks," I said. "Just another reason we're best friends."

"Oh," he said, "I almost forgot. My mom told me I had to tell your mom that I'm coming to the party. She said I had to do it early and then something about a recipe? Can I talk to her?"

I scratched my head. "Um, okay. I can't wait to see you. Hold on while I go wake her up."

"Okay," said Jo-Jo. "This party's going to be epic."

"Joseph-John!" A sharp voice called from the other end of the phone.

"Who's that?" I asked.

"Uh-oh," he said. "That's my mom and I think she means business."

"Joseph-John!" Her voice was louder now. "Are you on that phone? It's not even six o'clock."

"Reciping, Mom," said Jo-Jo. "Just like you said. And you said to do it as early as possible."

I could feel the tension through the phone.

"RSVP!" she said. "I asked you to RSVP! That's beside the point. Hang up that phone before you wake his entire family."

"Not his whole family," he said, "just Max and his mom. He's going to get her now."

"What?!" she shrieked.

I pulled the phone away from my ear and heard it clanking around on the other end.

"Hello? Max?" she said.

"Good morning, Jo-Jo's mom. Hold on just a second."

"Wait, Max!" she said. "Don't wake her. I'm sure you and Joseph-John are the only ones up at this hour. Please apologize to your parents for me."

"It's no problem," I said. "I'm so excited to see him today."

"I'm sure you're going to have a great time," she said. "Now please try to go back to sleep."

"I'll try, but I don't think it's going to work."

"Then try harder," she said, "and have a happy birthday."

"Thanks, Jo-Jo's mom. Goodbye."

I hung up the phone and leaned against the

kitchen counter. Now where was I? Hmm. That's right! How can I get my birthday wish to come true this year?

I drew in a deep breath and started concentrating, but I was interrupted by the creak of a door being opened. I peeked down the hall just as a light flickered on.

Chapter 2

Yuck! My Butt Is Wet!

I WAS SITTING on the kitchen floor with my eyes closed in concentration when Cody walked in.

"What are you doing, Max?" he asked. "And who was on the phone?"

"You heard that?"

He nodded. "How could I not?"

"It was Jo-Jo," I said. "He wanted to wish me a happy birthday."

"Figures," he said. "Why are you sitting out here in the dark?

I wiggled my toes in my soft slippers and looked at the ground. "I'm not going to tell you. You'll laugh."

"No, I won't," he said. "Come on. Tell me."

"I'm concentrating on my wish," I said. "I have to get it right this year."

"Oh brother," Cody said. "You're not still hooked

on *that,* are you? It's been the exact same thing every birthday and Christmas for as long as I can remember."

"Two Christmases and three birthdays to be exact," I said. "But it hasn't come true yet."

"Sure it did," Cody said. "It just got delivered to the wrong place."

I crossed my arms and glared at him. "That didn't count!"

"It *was* pretty weird when that little Chihuahua appeared in Hunny-G and G-Dude's backyard only days after you made your wish."

"They're lucky nobody claimed her even after we posted all those signs," I said. "I'm going to include my address this year."

Cody smiled.

"This is the year," I said. "I even kept my new goldfish, Walter, alive for six whole weeks, so I'm responsible."

"Taking care of a dog is way different than a fish," Cody said.

"I know," I said. "You can't even hug a fish. He squirmed out of my hands the last time I tried."

Cody looked at me funny.

"What?" I said. "Walter's fine. I wiped the carpet fuzz off and plopped him back in the bowl."

"No wonder that fish swims crooked," Cody said.

"You know, I hope you get that little Chihuahua this time. It would be fun to have a puppy."

I grabbed Cody by the shoulders.

"I've got a great idea!" I exclaimed. "You can help me wish for it! Two people wishing has to be more powerful than one."

"Hmm," he said. "Okay. It's the least I can do since it's your birthday and all."

He sat down beside me and crossed his legs.

"Okay, here goes," I said. "Just concentrate on happy Chihuahua thoughts."

"All right," he said. "Let's get this over with."

"Oh no!" I said. "I made last year's wish on a shooting star. We won't have enough wishing power inside the house."

We jumped to our feet and bolted to the window.

"It's still dark," I said, "but not for long."

"Might not see a shooting star, but we can find the brightest," Cody said.

"Let's go," I said, and we raced through the garage. I shut the door behind us and we were out in the cool night. We ran through the backyard, leaving a trail of footprints in the dew.

"Gross," I said as I sat down across from him. "The grass is wet."

"Stop complaining," Cody said. "This will only take a minute."

I scanned the sky until I found the brightest star.

"That one," I said, pointing. "Now close your eyes."

"I wish I may, I wish I might, have this wish I wish tonight," I said.

I peeked at Cody. His eyes were shut, so I began to whisper.

"Hello again," I said. "It's me, Max E. James. You probably already know my wish, but I don't think you heard it right last time."

I sat up straight and spoke clearly.

"I wish for a little white Chihuahua. A real living one, not a stuffed animal. And I want it delivered to my house this time, not to my grandparents' house or any other house. My address is One Dakota Street."

We sat for another minute in silence. I wanted to make sure it took this year.

I opened my eyes and tapped Cody's hand. "Okay," I said, "I think that did it. Let's go inside. My butt is wet."

We walked across the lawn toward the garage. When we reached the house, I accidentally slammed into Cody.

"Hey," I said. "Watch it. What are you doing?"

He spun around and leaned close to my face.

"Great, Max," he said.

"What?" I asked. "Open the door already."

Cody jiggled the door knob. "I can't."

CHAPTER 3

Bing-Bong!

CODY'S HEAD SLUMPED towards the ground as he shook it back and forth.

"Stop playing around and open the door," I said.

"I can't," he said. "You locked us out."

"Sor-ry," I said. "I guess I didn't check the lock."

"Guess not."

"What now?"

"We either have to wait outside until they wake up on their own, or we could try knocking on their window and see if they hear it. Great way to start your birthday, Max. I hope that wish of yours was worth it."

"Oh, it was worth it all right," I said.

"Hold on. Just let me think for a second."

The sun began to creep over the horizon as Cody mumbled to himself.

"Let's see," he said. "Maybe one of the windows is unlocked."

I walked right past him and stood at the door.

"We could ring the door bell," I said.

Bing-bong.

The chime pierced the morning silence.

"Max! What are you doing?"

"Ringing the doorbell," I said. "What does it look like?"

Bing-bong. Bing-bong.

"I'm not standing out here in the dark with a wet butt."

Bing-bong. Bing-bong. Bing-bong.

Cody grabbed my hand.

"Stop it!" he yelled. "They heard it the first time. All you're doing now is making them mad."

The lights flickered in the garage and a shadow appeared at the blinds. The corner lifted to reveal Mommy's sleepy face peering out. She stared at us, but didn't speak for what seemed like forever.

"Sorry," she said finally. "We don't want any!"

Cody's mouth dropped as she closed the blinds.

"I don't believe it," he said and lurched towards the door.

Bing-bong. Bing-bong. Bing-bong.

The door cracked open.

"What in the world are you two doing out here?" Mommy asked.

"Uh, I think you mean happy birthday!" I said with a huge smile.

"It's too early for your birthday," she said. "Now, someone needs to explain what's going on."

"It's like this," I said. "I wanted to make a wish

and needed a star to wish on. Cody said he'd help and then we found out the door locks automatically. Also, the grass is wet."

I pointed to the wet splotch on my rear.

"The good news," I said, "is that we made the wish."

Mommy's eyes shifted to Cody as her stone gaze cracked with a smile. She opened the door wider and waved us in.

"Today is going to be a busy day, gentlemen," she said. "Please let your father and me try to get a little more sleep. By the way, your grandparents will be here early this morning. We've got some running around to do before the party."

"All right!" I said. "I love when Hunny-G and G-Dude visit."

"We'll be quiet," Cody said.

"Thanks," she said. "And Max, who was that on the phone this morning?"

"Oh," I said. "You heard that?"

Mommy knelt down so we were face to face.

"I hear everything," she said.

"It was Jo-Jo," I said. "He was RSVPing and wishing me happy birthday."

"Well," she said, "that was very thoughtful of

him. To RSVP. At five in the morning. The day of the party."

"I also talked to Jo-Jo's Mom. She said she's sorry."

"Happy birthday, Max," she said. "I'm going back to bed."

Cody turned on the television as Mommy left.

"I don't want to watch TV," I said. "I want my birthday to start."

"Me too," he said. "But how can we make them want to get up?"

"Hmm. I've got it!" I said. "To the kitchen!"

CHAPTER 4

Breakfast in Bed

"THEY CAN'T RESIST breakfast in bed," I said.

"Terrific idea," Cody said. "So what's on the menu?"

I opened the pantry door and looked around. "How about pancakes?"

Cody frowned and shook his head. "No can do. The stove is off-limits. Don't you remember the flaming egg incident?"

I looked up at the yellow stains on the ceiling. "You're probably right."

"Besides, my allowance can't cover another new pan and we can't reach the batter," he said, pointing to the top shelf.

"Can we make them another way?" I asked. "What are pancakes made of?"

"Bread," Cody said. "Pancakes are basically just bread, right?"

"I like bread," I said. "That can be our main ingredient."

Cody smiled and pulled the loaf from the bread box. I grabbed a plate and he stacked our make-shift pancakes on it.

"All right," he said. "What else?"

"They need butter and syrup—and lots of it!"

I grabbed the butter and slathered it on both sides of each piece of bread. Cody doused the tower with syrup. It dripped down the sides of the sticky masterpiece.

"Oh, that looks yummy," I said. "Now what to drink?"

"Stinky coffee?" Cody asked.

"Sure, do you know how to make it?"

Cody shook his head. "No, but I know where the coffee beans are."

He opened a cabinet and pointed to the low-est shelf.

"Give me a boost and I'll get it," I said.

There were two containers, marked "ground" and "whole bean."

"Which one?" I asked, as I pulled the containers from the cabinet.

"Beats me," he said.

I climbed down and Cody set two mugs on the table. We stared for a few minutes.

"I know," I said. "Let's use both!"

"Sounds good to me."

Cody spooned both types of coffee into each mug.

"How many scoops?"

"Maybe three each?" I said.

"If you say so."

Cody added water to each cup and stirred. He peeked into the cup, frowned, and stirred faster.

"It's not dissolving," he said. "Look at all the floaters."

"You have to cook it," I said. "Coffee is hot."

I opened the microwave door and Cody put in the mugs. I pressed start and watched the mugs spin around and around. At the three minute mark they bubbled over, so we took them out.

"They're still floating," I said, poking a bean on the surface.

"Well, it stinks like coffee," Cody said.

I plucked a bean out with my fingers. "Ouch!" I screamed. "That's hot."

"What are you doing?"

"Picking out the floaters."

Cody shook his head and handed me a spoon. "Use this."

I fished them out one by one. "There," I said. "That's more like it."

"You ready?" Cody said.

"Let's go."

I led the way down the hall as Cody balanced the tray behind me. I pushed Mommy and Daddy's bedroom door open and flipped on the light.

"Yay!" I shouted. "Breakfast in bed for you and happy birthday to me!"

CHAPTER 5

Open Wide for the Airplane

CODY SET THE tray down at the foot of the bed and we waited in silence. Daddy peeked at us through one squinty eye. Mommy disappeared under the blankets.

"A-hem," I said. "Happy birthday to me!"

"We made you breakfast in bed," said Cody. "Time to get up."

The covers drew tighter around Mommy's head and Daddy rubbed his eyes.

"Happy birthday, Max," he said, sitting up and tugging the covers off of Mommy.

"What do you have there, boys?" he asked. "Looks interesting."

"Pancakes and coffee," I said. "We made them

all by ourselves and we didn't even use the stove. Drink up," Cody said as he handed some coffee to Daddy.

Daddy peered into his mug and his eyes widened.

"Might want to go easy on that, Honey," he said. "Looks like some pretty strong brew."

Mommy swirled her cup and sniffed it. Her lip curled every time the mug neared her mouth.

"Go ahead, Mommy," I said. "Take a sip."

Daddy joined in.

"Yes, Mommy," he said. "Tell us how it is."

Mommy squinted her eyes at Daddy and slurped a tiny sip from the mug. She coughed and pulled the cup away.

"Whew!" she said. "It's certainly the most interesting coffee I've tasted. And it's a bit crunchy."

"Don't you like it?" I asked.

"I do, Max," she said. "It's just a little strong for my taste."

She put her cup down and we turned our attention to Daddy. He took a gulp and smiled.

"I like strong coffee," he said. His smile revealed coffee grounds lodged between his teeth.

"Ahhh," he said. "Delightful."

Mommy pointed to the plate. "And these are what again?"

"Pancakes," Cody said.

"Wonderful," she said. "That's Daddy's favorite." She cut a huge forkful.

"Here you go, Sweetie," she said, lifting it to his mouth. "Open wide for the airplane! *Brrrrrrrr.*"

Mommy stuffed the entire bite into Daddy's

mouth. His eyes opened wide and his cheeks ballooned out like a chipmunk as the buttery syrup mixture ran down his chin. We stared at him waiting for his response.

"That's something," he said.

"How was it?" Cody asked.

Mommy handed him his coffee mug. "Wash it down with this," she said.

"Very good, boys," he said. "I'd go lighter on the butter next time, but it wasn't bad."

She giggled and forked another huge bite.

"Ready for more," she asked.

"You're so thoughtful, Honey, but that one's for you. The boys went through a lot of effort to make this for us," said Daddy.

She lifted her fork to her mouth, and nibbled like a mouse.

"Oh, that is good," she said. "Thank you boys. Now listen, we have a lot to do today. Daddy and I are going to get dressed. We'll be out in a minute."

My face went sour.

"What do you mean a lot to do?" I said. "It's my birthday. The only thing I have to do today is turn seven."

"We've got to pick up the cake, get the balloons, decorate, and prepare the food," she said.

"Come on, Max," Cody said. "Let's go find something else to do."

We plopped down on the couch in a huff. As we turned on the television, the door bell rang: *Bing-bong. Bing-bong.*

CHAPTER 6

Ice Cream for What?

CODY AND I ran to the door and pulled back the blinds.

"Hey," I said. "It's Hunny-G and G-Dude James!"

"Happy Birthday, Max!" they said as the door swung open. "And happy non-birthday to you, Cody."

We grabbed their bags and brought them into the house.

"Come on," I said. "Now the party can officially start."

"How old are you today, seventeen?" G-Dude asked. "I keep forgetting and you're getting so big."

"No silly, I'm only seven," I said. "But I did grow two whole inches."

"Maybe that's it," said G-Dude.

"I hear there's a party today. Are you excited?" Hunny-G said.

"Yes, but we have to wait like thirty hours before it starts and Mommy said we have stuff to do first. Mommy! Daddy! Hunny-G and G-Dude are here!" I yelled, heading into the kitchen. Mommy and Daddy were washing the breakfast dishes.

"Boy," I said. "You guys sure were hungry."

"Yeah," said Cody, "Your plates are spotless."

"It really hit the spot," Daddy said. "Hunny-G, did you know that Max and Cody made breakfast for us this morning?"

"That's precious, boys" said Hunny-G James. "I remember the breakfasts your father used to make us."

"Bet they weren't as good as ours," said Cody.

"No, probably not," she said. "But it's the thought that counts. Some were certainly interesting."

G-Dude stuck his finger in his mouth and acted like he was gagging. "They were great," he said.

Daddy smiled as he took out the trash.

"All right," said Mommy. "Time to go get dressed. You guys are going to go out with your grandparents while we get ready for the party."

"Sounds good to me," I said.

"Loving it," Cody said.

We dressed and were back in the kitchen just in time to catch the last part of Mommy's conversation with Hunny-G.

"Sure," said Hunny-G. "We'd love to pick up the ice cream cake."

"Cake?" My mouth watered. If there's one thing I love, it's ice cream cake. "What are we waiting for?" I asked. "Let's get a move on, people."

"Race you to the car," G-Dude said, already halfway out the door.

Cody and I took off after him.

"Guess that's my cue," Hunny-G said.

We were already buckled up when she got into the car.

Growl!

"What was that?" G-Dude asked. "Is there a bear back there?"

I grabbed my stomach. "No," I said. "Our parents ate, but we didn't. I'm starving."

"That's something we'll have to take care of," said G-Dude. "Let's go get that cake."

"Wait," I said. "We're going to pick up the cake before breakfast?"

"Well, isn't it your birthday?" Hunny-G asked.

"Yes," I said.

"And isn't it your non-birthday, Cody?" she asked.

"Sure is," he said.

"Sounds like a good day to have ice cream for breakfast to me," said G-Dude.

We zoomed off. The ice cream shop was four songs away from our house when Daddy drove, but with G-Dude driving we made it in just over three! It seemed like the louder we sang, the faster G-Dude drove.

When the car came to a halt, Cody and I swung open the doors and sprinted to the shop. We pulled open the door and were greeted by the sweet smell of freshly baked waffle cones. The shop was empty except for the mesmerizing ice cream colors lining the freezer. We pressed our faces against the glass.

"Good morning," said the lady behind the counter.

I could barely contain myself.

"Double-chunk, chocolate-chip fudge cone, please," I said.

She raised her eyebrows and smiled. "Isn't it a bit early for ice cream?"

"It's my birthday and this is breakfast!"

"In that case, happy birthday," she said. "I'll be sure to give you a big scoop."

"Same for me, please," Cody said.

G-Dude and Hunny-G ordered ice cream and we took a seat by the window.

"Yum." I licked the chocolate ice cream. "This is the best."

I looked at Cody. Chocolate dripped from his chin. He smiled and continued to lap the ice cream.

The lady from behind the counter placed a large, flat box on the table in front of us.

"Do you want a peek?" she asked.

"My cake!" I said.

We opened the box and there it was. A chocolate and vanilla ice cream cake with a picture of a huge Chihuahua across the top.

"Wow," I said. "It looks so good. I want to eat it right now."

Hunny-G snapped the box shut as I reached in for a quick taste test.

Cody and G-Dude laughed.

"Ouch," I said. "You almost got my finger."

"Well," Hunny-G said. "You almost touched the cake." She waved her finger back and forth. "Not until the party. Your mother would be very upset if we brought home a cake with fingerprints on it."

I smiled and went back to my ice cream cone.

"So, Max. What did you wish for this year?" asked G-Dude.

"You already know," I said.

"Oh brother, here we go again," Cody said.

"We do?" Hunny-G asked.

"Yes," I said. "It was accidentally delivered to your house last winter."

"Oh, that!" Hunny-G said. "And we are so

thankful for your little Chihuahua. We love her very much. You know you can visit anytime you like."

"Thanks," I said. "But I want my own."

"Well, speaking of birthday presents," she said. "G-Dude and I have your gift in the car. Your parents said we could give it to you before the party."

"Would you like it now?" G-Dude asked.

"Would I?" I said. I nodded my head up and down.

"Well, finish your ice cream and let's go get it," G-Dude said.

CHAPTER 7

I Know It's Plastic

WE GRABBED THE cake and headed for the car.

"You two get buckled in," G-Dude said. He put the cake in the in the passenger seat and popped the trunk. "I'll be right back."

"Close your eyes," Hunny-G said. "And don't peek."

We shut our eyes real tight. I couldn't wait to see it.

"Birthday presents, my favorite!" I scrunched my eyes even tighter.

The trunk thumped closed and I heard footsteps. I bit down on my lip and opened an eye.

"Okay, Max," called Hunny-G. "Do you still have your eyes closed?"

"Yes," I said.

She placed a gift bag on my lap.

Yip, yip. Howl, howl.

Something was crying from inside the bag.

I couldn't believe my ears. Had my birthday wish come true? Wait, I thought. How could a dog breathe in the trunk all this time?

I opened my eyes and tore open the bag. I reached in, expecting something soft and warm, but it was cold and hard. It was a robotic Chihuahua.

"Surprise!" they screamed.

"Your parents wouldn't let us get you a real one, so we figured this was the next best thing," Hunny-G said.

Yip, yip. Howl, howl.

"Gee, thanks," I said. "I think I'll name her Chloe." I looked up and forced a big smile.

"I know you had your heart set on a real dog, Max," she said, "but rules are rules."

"Well, when I grow up, my kids won't have any rules!"

Hunny-G looked at G-Dude and said softly, "We're not babysitting for him."

G-Dude smiled and shook his head.

"Can I see it?" Cody asked.

I handed it over.

On the way home, Cody discovered that a pat

on the head made Chloe bark and she walked when you tugged on her leash.

I turned to Cody. "I did say real Chihuahua this morning, right?"

"I think so," he said, "but maybe not."

We pulled into the driveway and were surprised to see a strange car.

"I wonder who that could be," I said. "Is it party time?"

"No," Cody said. "We've got at least another hour. Someone is early."

G-Dude's car had barely stopped when I burst out the door and ran into the house.

Sitting in my kitchen were Jo-Jo and his mom. "Sweet!" I screamed.

"Happy birthday, Max," Jo-Jo's mom said. "Again."

"Yeah, happy birthday," Jo-Jo said. He threw his arms around me and gave me a huge birthday hug.

The rest of the bunch trailed in behind me and placed Chloe and the cake on the table.

"Ooooh," Jo-Jo said. "Cool dog. Is that the cake?"

"Check it out," I said. I showed him all the tricks Chloe could do and then looked up at Mommy. "She's not real, but I'm still holding out hope."

"That's precious," said Jo-Jo's mom as she turned back to Mommy. "Are you sure it's okay?"

"Absolutely. No need to worry. We love having Jo-Jo over," she said.

Jo-Jo whispered in my ear. "I accidentally told my mom the wrong party time. I was so excited this morning."

"That's okay," I said. "This is a great birth-day surprise."

"Thanks again for understanding," said Jo-Jo's mom. "I'm sorry about the mix up." She looked at Jo-Jo. "Best behavior, right, Joseph-John?"

"Yes ma'am," he said. "See you later, Mom."

She kissed him on the forehead and waved goodbye.

"Okay, boys," Mommy said. "I have a lot to do, so I need you to entertain yourselves—preferably outside."

I looked at Cody and Jo-Jo.

"I know what we can do!" I shouted. "Only we need a grown-up for pushing power."

Almost at once, everyone turned and looked at G-Dude.

"Uh, I guess I can go out with the boys," he said.

"Great idea," Mommy said.

We walked out the back door onto the deck. I pointed. "There," I said.

It swayed in the light breeze, dangling between two tall trees. We sprinted off the deck all trying to reach it first.

"Hey, guys," called G-Dude. "Wait for me!"

Chapter 8

Tummy Butters

WE WERE OFF the deck in a flash and at the base of two billowing pine trees in seconds. Between them, a tire swing hung from a long yellow rope. Jo-Jo and I leapt onto the swing and G-Dude began pushing slowly. Cody would have to wait his turn.

"Higher," I said. "I want tummy butters."

Jo-Jo looked at me strangely. "What are tummy butters?"

"You know, like when your guts feel like they're going to come out of your mouth," I said. "Sort of like when an elevator drops really quick."

Jo-Jo grew quiet.

"Hold on tight," G-Dude said.

He pulled the tire swing back and sprinted beneath it, shoving it over his head as he ran. We went so high that we were looking straight at the ground as we came down! My stomach dropped and Jo-Jo's knuckles were white from the death-grip he had on the chains.

"Ahhhhh!" He screamed all the way down.

"Are you okay?" I asked.

He turned and grinned. "Tummy butters!"

Cody leaned against a tree and twirled his finger slowly in the air. "Wow, so high."

G-Dude kept pushing, but Cody grew tired of watching us have all the fun.

"It's my turn now," he said. "Let's do the spinning tire of doom."

The swing came to a stop and Jo-Jo and I got off. Cody slid onto it belly first. He held a chain under each arm and one between his legs.

"Here we go," G-Dude said.

He pulled chain after chain, spinning Cody in a circle and gaining speed as he went. Cody's legs flung about as he spun.

"Wait until you see what happens when he stands up, Jo-Jo. It's going to be great."

It wasn't long before Cody was ready to get off.

"Okay," Cody said. "I'm done." His face was beginning to lose color.

The swing slowed, but it didn't look like he could focus as he stared off into space. The swing stopped as Cody grasped for the earth beneath him before trying to stand.

I picked up a long stick and walked toward him.

He wobbled and stumbled forward with his head tilted at a funny angle. That's when I tripped him. He fell flat on the ground.

"Ooof," he said as he hit.

Jo-Jo and I erupted with laughter.

"That wasn't nice, Max," G-Dude said.

"Yeah, but it sure was funny," I said.

Cody managed to sit up. "Don't worry. What goes around, comes around."

"Whatever," I said and turned my attention to G-Dude. "What time is it? It has to be close to party time by now."

Before he could answer, I heard the clang of a car door closing. A short figure approached.

"Yay!" I said. "Over here, Jacob."

I waved my hands and jumped in the air. He ran over to the tire swing and greeted us.

"Hey, guys," he said. "Happy birthday, Max."

Jacob is my second best friend. We were in first grade together, but have different second grade teachers. Now I only see him during recess or play dates.

Next, Herby arrived. We're on the same soccer team. He's my third best friend.

"Hey, Herby," I said. "How's it going?"

"Great, Max," he said. "Happy birthday. Hey, Jacob. What's up, Jo-Jo."

"Wow," I said. "Everyone I invited came!"

"Okay, boys," said G-Dude. "Time to use kid-power on this thing. I'm pooped."

He walked back to the deck and we all took turns pushing each other. Even Cody joined in.

"So what's the plan for the party?" Jacob asked. "Will there be games?"

"I'm not sure," I said. "My parents said they have stuff planned, but wouldn't tell me what."

Just then, we heard another car door.

Cody looked up and smiled, apparently recognizing the car. He nudged me with his elbow.

"Mommy let me invite a friend of my own," he said.

"What?!" I said. "No fair! It's not even your party. Who did you invite?"

"Seamus," he said.

I frowned at him. "You better not bother us. Just remember whose birthday it is."

Cody ran over to greet him.

"He better have a present!" I yelled.

Herby tugged at my sleeve and pointed towards the deck. "Is that part of the party?" he asked.

I turned to see Daddy and G-Dude making their way onto the lawn. They had something in their hands, but I couldn't tell what it was.

MAX E. JAMES

BIRTHDAY BASH
PART 2

J. RYAN HERSEY

Illustrated by Gustavo Mazali

MAX E. JAMES

BIRTHDAY BASH

PART 2

J. RYAN HERSEY

Illustrated by Gustavo Mazali

To my good friend, Britt – may the
commute always be long.

CHAPTER 1

Let's Get This Party Started!

G-DUDE AND DADDY were carrying something wrapped in a tarp. I wondered what it could be. And what was that rope for?

Daddy tossed the rope over a tree branch. G-Dude caught it on the other side.

Jo-Jo appeared beside me, ready to investigate. We walked toward G-Dude and Daddy.

"What are they doing, Max?" he asked, keeping pace with me.

"I don't know," I said.

As we approached, G-Dude pulled on the rope and the tarp fell away.

A giant head with huge eyes rose into the air. Its

long, pink tongue dangled in the wind while G-Dude tied it off about head height.

"Wow," I said. "Look at that!"

Jo-Jo didn't say anything. He just stared at the papier-mâché masterpiece.

I tapped him on the shoulder.

"That's the coolest piñata I've ever seen," he said.

"Yeah," I said. "That Chihuahua head is almost as big as I am."

Everyone ran up to us as the piñata spun slowly. It seemed to scan the party with its huge bug eyes.

"All right, if we're going to do this, everyone get behind this line," he said, scratching a line in the dirt under the giant Chihuahua head. "I need everyone right here, lined up from smallest to biggest."

He pointed with the stick and the eager line wriggled like a snake as it formed. Mommy handed everyone a plastic bag.

"You may need these," she said.

I worked my way to the front of the line. Not only was it my birthday, but I was also the smallest of the bunch.

"Yay," I said. "I'm first!"

G-Dude spread the blue tarp beneath the piñata. I could actually feel the excitement as I stepped forward.

I marveled at it for a minute. The huge ears made it look just like a real Chihuahua. Its tongue dangled toward the ground—it made a wonderful target.

I grabbed the stick and wound up, but Daddy caught it before I could swing.

"Hold on a second," he said.

He pulled a strip of black cloth from his pocket. "Not without a blindfold. This has to last at least one round."

Reluctantly, I allowed him to tie it around my head. When he finished, I couldn't see a thing.

He spun me around five times and told me to swing. I could hear whispers and giggles from behind me. I took a deep breath and swung with all my might.

CHAPTER 2

Swinging for the Fences

SWISH!

My stick sliced through the air but hit nothing. The crowd giggled as I pulled off the blindfold. The piñata had vanished.

"Behind you," Cody said. He pointed over my shoulder.

"Very funny," I said.

"Okay," Daddy said. "We'll give him another chance since it's his birthday."

He re-tied the blindfold and spun me around again. I tightened my grip and stretched the stick out in front of me. I wiggled it back and forth until I found the piñata. Not going to miss you this time, I thought. I drew back and let it fly.

Swish!

I missed again.

"What!?" I screamed, tearing off the blindfold.

G-Dude greeted me with a smile and pointed up with his eyes. The piñata hung above me, well out of my reach.

"Hey! No fair," I said.

He lowered the piñata back down.

"We're just kidding," Daddy said. "We won't move it again." He put the blindfold back on.

"All right, Max," he said. "Try it now."

I swung as hard as I could. I didn't even wait this time.

Crack!

My hands stung from the vibrating stick.

"There must be a lot of candy in there," Herby said. "It barely moved."

"About twenty pounds by my estimate," said G-Dude.

Jo-Jo was next in line.

"Get ready," he said. "I'm going to whack it."

He swung the stick back and forth as Daddy adjusted the blindfold from behind.

Thwack!

He struck it in the same spot as me – the dent was visible now.

Jacob went next. Then Herby took his turn. Both had solid hits, but didn't do much damage. Cody and Seamus went last. Not only were they the biggest, but they also played baseball.

Cody walked up first and sized up the piñata. He spun it around so that the dent was right in front then Daddy blindfolded him.

Faah-whaap!

A piece of the ear sailed through the air, but no candy fell out.

Everyone giggled and slowly crept toward the tarp.

"Not yet," Daddy said. "Stay behind the line."

Cody handed the stick to Seamus, who looked like he was stepping up to home plate to swing for the fences.

Whack!

Without warning, he struck the piñata so hard that Herby almost jumped out of his skin.

"Okay," Daddy said. "Now everyone gets a second hit."

The line started over and I noticed a small crack on one side. My second attempt convinced a single piece of candy to fall out. I grabbed it, handed the stick to Jo-Jo, and headed to the end of the line.

"Now we're really getting somewhere," Jo-Jo said.

"I can almost taste the candy," Jacob said.

The onslaught continued as piñata pieces continued to fall away. The tongue lay on the ground beneath the twirling head. You could hardly tell it was a Chihuahua anymore. The good news was that the crack had grown.

By the time it was Cody's turn, candy was dribbling out with every hit.

"You got this," Seamus said.

Without hesitation, Cody swung and a bunch of candy fell to the ground.

The kids rushed onto the tarp to retrieve it.

"Wait, wait, wait," Daddy said. "Not yet."

He tried to maintain order, but it was hard to do with all the bubble gum, lollipops, and chocolate bars scattered across the tarp. My mouth watered.

We all knew the next hit would release the sweet treasure. Cody carefully lined up the stick and unloaded with all his might. Instantly, a shower of color exploded before us as the orderly line erupted into chaos.

CHAPTER 3

Candy Doesn't Have a Tax

A SQUEAL PIERCED the air as the avalanche of sweets spread across the tarp.

"Candy!" someone screamed. Daddy jumped out of the way just before we dove into the mound.

I worked my way in and grabbed all the chocolate and bubble gum I could find.

In what seemed like seconds, the heaping pile was reduced to a few empty wrappers and broken pieces.

"Wow," Herby said, lifting his bulging bag. "That's a lot of candy."

Jo-Jo frantically unwrapped piece after piece and devoured chocolate bars and gummy treats. Chocolate dripped from the corners of his mouth as he stuffed them in.

"Easy," Jacob said. "You don't want to get a stomach ache."

Over Jo-Jo's shoulder I noticed Daddy and the other grown-ups walking into the yard carrying plastic grocery bags. I was just about to call after them when I heard Cody yell, "Candy tax!"

Seamus and Cody were working their way through the party, going through everyone's bag.

"Candy tax?" Herby asked. "What are you two blabbing about now?"

Cody grinned. "We did most of the work, so we should get most of the candy."

Seamus nodded in agreement. "It's our tax for breaking it. If it wasn't for us, you wouldn't have anything."

I scanned the yard for some grown-up support, but there was none to be found. They were still scattering grocery bags throughout the backyard. We'd have to face this on our own.

I looked back at Cody.

"You don't get a candy tax," I said. "We all helped bust the piñata."

"Candy tax!" Cody said, leaning in closer to me.

"I got your tax right here," I said.

I reached into my bag, pulled out a wrapper, and dropped it in his hand. I don't think he liked that because he shoved his hand into my bag and pawed through it. I grabbed his wrist with both hands and sank to the ground.

Jo-Jo pounced on his legs.

"Oh, no you don't," he said, wrapping around him like an octopus. "You're not getting a single piece of his candy."

Cody almost had his hand free when Mommy walked by.

"Um," she said, "what are you boys doing?"

"They're taxing our candy!" I screamed.

Cody looked up and smiled.

"I was just trying to share with the birthday boy," he said.

"Sure, Cody," she said. "Let him go. There was twenty pounds of candy in that piñata – plenty for everyone."

He let go then he smiled at me with a twinkle in his eyes. Something told me that this wasn't over yet.

I looked him dead in the eye, took a step forward, and tilted my head to one side.

Just as I was about to open my mouth, Daddy and the other grown-ups appeared. Their faces glistened in the sun.

"Man," Daddy said. "That was hard work."

"What are you talking about?" I asked.

Daddy pointed at the yard, which was littered with bulging grocery bags.

Everyone looked out across the sea of bags. Nobody knew quite what to say, because we didn't know what we were looking at.

"What's so great about bags?" I asked.

"Oh, my son," he said. "It's not the bags. It's what's in them."

CHAPTER 4

What's in the Bags?

"WHAT'S IN THE bags?" I asked.

"Okay, kids," Daddy said, ignoring me. "Go get your bathing suits on."

Everyone scattered but me.

"You too, Max," he said. "You don't want to miss this."

I scowled and ran into the house. Jo-Jo, Herby, and Jacob were already piled in my room and furiously changing into their suits.

My mind raced as we changed in silence. It could be squirt guns, I thought. Maybe sprinklers? No, not in bags. How would they sprinkle?

We spilled out the door onto the deck where Seamus and Cody were already waiting.

"Okay," Daddy said. "Is everyone here?"

"Yes!" we screamed.

"All right then," he said. "Take a seat and I'll explain the rules." He pointed to the steps leading to the deck.

We looked out across the backyard at the lumpy grocery bags. Their sides bulged like sacks of potatoes.

I elbowed Herby. "Do you see colors? It looks like they're filled with something colorful."

I raised my hand.

"Excuse me," I said.

"Yes, Max."

"What's in the bags?"

"Yeah!" everyone screamed. "Tell us!"

Daddy smiled as he revealed a perfect globe. He held it high above his head and dropped it. The sun sparkled through its clear blue skin just before it exploded at his feet.

"Water balloons!" he screamed.

Everybody jumped to their feet and cheered. We started down the stairs, but Daddy stopped us.

"Whoa, whoa, whoa," he said. "Rules first."

We could barely contain ourselves, like a dam ready to overflow.

"Who wants to throw water balloons?" he shouted.

Everyone screamed, "I do!"

"Great," he said. "Then you're also willing to get hit. Right?"

"Yeah!" we all screamed.

"Okay," he said. "Don't pick up the bags." Daddy's eyes shifted to Cody and Seamus. "And no ganging up."

We all nodded, but out of the corner of my eye I caught Cody winking at Seamus.

I stuck my tongue out at Cody. He just smiled and blew me a kiss.

"Does anybody have any questions?" Daddy asked.

"No!" everyone yelled.

"Well," he said. "Why are you guys still sitting around?"

Chapter 5

Double Teamed

WE WERE OFF like a shot sprinting toward the bags. The first one I opened was filled with water balloons of all different colors. I grabbed a few and looked for my first victim.

"Look out!" Jo-Jo said. I turned to look and felt a balloon whiz past my head before splashing on the ground beside me.

"Whoa," I said. "That was close. Who threw that?"

It was no use. A rainbow of water balloons littered the sky as kids ran in all directions. I bent down to reload and was hit in the stomach.

"Ugh," I said. "These things are not as soft as they look."

"I know," Jo-Jo said. He pulled up his shirt to reveal a red splotch.

Seamus and Cody were doubled over with laughter, pointing at us.

"Direct hit," I heard Cody say.

"Let's get them!" Jo-Jo said.

Herby and Jacob ran by and I grabbed them.

"You guys want to help us get Cody and Seamus?"

They nodded.

"Those two have it coming," Jacob said.

We grabbed as many water balloons as we could carry and ran in their direction. Cody spotted us and signaled Seamus.

They began firing and balloons exploded all around us as we ran.

A pink balloon whooshed by my head, then I took one on the knee. I turned to see Herby get blasted in the chest. He dropped every balloon he was carrying.

One slammed directly into Jo-Jo's stomach and he went down too.

"Man down! Man down!" Jacob cried as he stopped to assist the fallen.

Now he was a sitting duck and our attackers knew it. They unleashed a flurry of strikes as fast as they could throw. Jo-Jo and Jacob never had a chance.

It was up to me now. I ran through the barrage, clutching four water balloons. They jiggled as I dodged throws. It was only when I reached them that I realized my back-up was gone. I turned to see my posse running in the opposite direction. Surely they would return with reinforcements. I just had to hold my ground until then.

I stopped within firing range. Cody walked closer.

"Okay, Max," he said. "Take your best shot."

"Yeah," Seamus said. He leaned forward and pointed to his chin.

I lobbed one at Cody. He leaned in just before it connected. It breezed past his cheek and burst on the ground. The next one did the same.

Cody laughed and Seamus stepped forward.

"Two left," Seamus said. "Better make them count."

I threw them both as hard as I could, but they fell short and splashed at his feet. His grin grew as Cody handed him a bag of balloons.

"Hey," I said, looking around for the nearest place to reload. "That's against the rules!"

"We're going to make an exception for you," Cody said.

I tried to run, but stumbled and crashed to the

ground. I managed to roll onto my back, but they were upon me.

All I could see were their smiling faces as the sun shone through the water balloons they held.

"Well, well, well," Seamus said. "What do we have here?"

"I don't know," Cody said. "Looks like someone in trouble to me."

My heart pounded and a lump grew in my throat – they were not going to go easy on me.

Cody dropped one onto my forehead. The cool water drenched my head and some even got up my nose. It made me cough.

"Oh, I'm sorry," Cody said. "I must have dropped that one. I'm so clumsy."

Seamus released one onto my chest next. He laughed as it exploded and soaked my shirt.

"Hey!" I said, propping myself up on my elbows. "This isn't fair. It's two against one and I don't have any ammo."

I scanned the yard for my cavalry, but I was alone.

"You're right," Cody said. "We'll give you a head start."

Before I had time to react, they started counting.

"One. Two!" they shouted and unloaded water balloons on me as I tried to crawl away.

I tried to duck and cover, but they were coming too fast. Colors rained down on my head and back. It lasted for what seemed like forever, then, as quick as it began, it was over.

"Out of water balloons," Seamus said.

And just like that, they disappeared.

I lay in a puddle of muddy water and pride. I rolled onto my back and leaned my head into the slop. That's when I saw a shadow.

"Wow," Jo-Jo said. "They really got you."

I looked up. Herby and Jacob were standing beside Jo-Jo.

"Thanks a lot, guys," I said. "Where were you?"

"We went to reload and got ambushed by your dad," Jo-Jo said.

"He throws hard," Herby said, rubbing his back.

"Yeah," Jacob said. "We got back as quick as we could, but it was too late."

They pulled me up from the mud.

"Boy," Jacob said. "There isn't a dry spot on you."

"Thanks for noticing," I said as we walked to the next bag of balloons. "They have to pay."

"Hey. "Where are Seamus and Cody going?" Jo-Jo asked.

There was a row of bushes at the back of the yard. Cody and Seamus ducked behind them.

"They're stashing water balloons," I said. "That's cheating."

We walked toward them.

"Whoa," Herby cried, crashing to the ground.

We lifted him up. There was something tangled around his feet.

"Dumb piñata rope," he said, kicking it off.

I smiled and picked it up.

"Bring it in boys," I said. "It's payback time."

CHAPTER 6

Payback Time

I TORE THE last bit of piñata from the rope and snapped it taught.

"All right," I said. "Here's what we're going to do."

They huddled around and I explained my plan. It was a dangerous mission, but smiles grew wide on their faces as they listened carefully.

"Okay," I said as I coiled the rope and put it in the rear of my pants. "Ready?"

They nodded.

"Only one thing left to decide," I said. "Who's the bait?"

They all looked down at their feet and shuffled them in the grass.

"I'll do it," Jo-Jo said and stepped forward.

"You're a good man," I said. "You won't be forgotten."

I handed him two plump water balloons. Jo-Jo nodded and smiled.

I turned to Herby and Jacob who each had two full bags of water balloons.

"Are you guys ready?" I asked.

"Ready as I'll ever be," Herby said.

"Yup," Jacob said.

We stepped into the open at the perfect time. Seamus and Cody were in the middle of a battle with Daddy and G-Dude, so they didn't see us creep up from behind.

"Now's our chance," I said. "Go, Jo-Jo!"

He took off toward Seamus at full speed. The water balloons jiggled in his hands. Seamus turned back toward the bushes and Jo-Jo slammed a pink water balloon into his face. The blast drenched him instantly. Before he could react, Jo-Jo chucked another one. It hit him square in the chest.

"Take that!" he screamed and sped away.

Seamus grabbed a bag of balloons and took off after him.

Luckily for us, Cody didn't see the exchange and his back was still to us. Jacob and Herby attacked as he ducked behind the bushes to reload.

Cody was so caught up with them, he didn't notice

me slip behind the other side of the bushes. I pulled the rope from my pants and crawled toward him.

I slipped the rope around his feet and screamed, "Get him!"

Jacob and Herby tackled Cody and pinned him to the ground. I furiously wrapped the rope around his legs as he lay thrashing, and tied his feet together with my very best knot.

"You guys better let me go," he said. "Or else."

"Or else what?" Herby said. "Looks like you aren't going anywhere to me."

"Yeah," Jacob said. "We got you now!"

We stood above him admiring our handiwork as he struggled to free his legs.

"Don't worry, Cody," I whispered, reaching into the bag. "I triple-knotted it."

We pelted him with water balloons. They exploded all over him.

Cody couldn't decide whether to cover his face or untie the rope. He flailed his arms from his face to his feet and back again.

"Take that!" I shouted. "How do you like it?"

Herby and Jacob continued throwing, and the puddle surrounding Cody grew. That's when I saw a blur of color out of the corner of my eye – it was Jo-Jo! He sprinted by and smashed a balloon right into Cody's face with great delight.

"Time to get moving, guys," he said between deep breaths. "Seamus is hot on my tail."

We looked up and saw him running toward us, lobbing balloons as he approached.

"Let him go," he yelled. "Get off of him!"

Laughing with delight, we all got up and ran. As I turned, I slammed into something and fell backwards. It was Daddy. I looked up at his scowling face.

CHAPTER 7

Ice Cream and Cake

I BOUNCED OFF his legs and fell to the ground.

"I can explain," I said, grinning.

"I'm sure you can," he said.

I opened my mouth to speak and a water balloon slammed into my back. The explosion sprayed Daddy's shirt.

"Ouch!" I said, rubbing my back.

Seamus stood behind me with another balloon locked and loaded.

"How do you like it?" he asked.

Daddy leaned to one side of us to get a better look at the soggy boy lumped on the ground.

Cody was still trying to untie his feet.

"They did it first!" I screamed.

Daddy looked at Cody.

"Is that true?"

"It is," Jo-Jo said, joining the group. "They ganged up on Max."

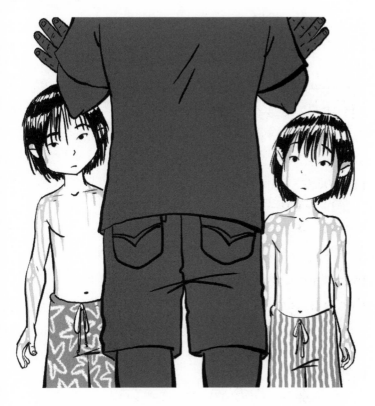

"Cody?" he asked again.

"Well, yes," he said, "but we were just having fun."

"You bombarded me!" I screamed.

"We gave you a head start," Cody said, now standing.

I frowned and felt my cheeks getting hot. "Two seconds isn't a head start!"

"All of you broke my rules," Daddy said. "Including you guys." He pointed to Herby, Jacob, and Jo-Jo, who were slinking away.

"True," Seamus said. "But it was all in good fun and nobody got hurt. Right, Max?"

"I guess so," I said.

Cody was soaked from head to toe. He lifted his shirt to reveal a bunch of welts on his stomach.

"I'd say it was pretty even," he said. He put his hand on my shoulder and patted me on the back. "I can appreciate a good water balloon strike."

"Well," Daddy said, "Did you have fun?"

"Yes!" we all yelled.

"I guess we can let it go," he said. "But no more ganging up on people. Now you boys pick up the empty bags."

We all took off through the yard and grabbed bags as we went. We threw any straggling water balloons we found.

Mommy appeared on the deck minutes later with a pile of towels. "Dry off and change your clothes. Then we'll have ice cream and cake."

"Oh no," I said. In all the fun, I had forgotten

my wish. My heart sank a little, but there was no time for that. I had one more chance.

I sprinted into the house to change. My friends followed and were back outside in a flash.

On our way out, I noticed the pile of birthday presents in the living room.

"I have to make this one count," I said as we walked onto the deck.

Jo-Jo heard me muttering to myself. "Make what count?" he asked.

"My birthday wish," I said. "The candles are my last shot and I have to make them count. One breath, I have to do it in one breath."

CHAPTER 8

That Takes Care of You

MOMMY UNVEILED THE cake and placed seven candles around the face of the Chihuahua.

"Careful of the eyes, Mommy!" I said.

She lit each one as I reached for the corner of the cake.

"Don't touch that cake, Max. Not until we sing 'Happy Birthday' and even then don't stick your fingers in it."

I batted my eyes and lowered my hand. I took a huge breath in. The frosting smelled wonderful.

"Everyone gather round," Mommy said.

We stepped closer.

"One. Two. Three," she said and then raised her arms and conducted the group.

The crowd erupted with the lyrics of "Happy Birthday" as the candles flickered.

"Happy birthday to you, cha, cha, cha. Happy birthday to you, cha, cha, cha," echoed through the yard.

The singing faded into the background as I focused on the candles. I had to harness all my wishing power in one giant blow. If I could extinguish them in a single breath, maybe my wish would come true. All I could think of was a cute little Chihuahua. That was all I wanted.

I snapped back to the moment. They were on the last verse, so I took a huge breath. As I inhaled, my lungs burned and felt as if they would burst, like an over-filled balloon. I took my last sip of air, just as the final note trailed off.

"Blow out your candles, Max," someone yelled.

I blew so hard I thought the candles might fly off the cake. Luckily that didn't happen. All that was left were trails of smoke where the flames had been.

Everyone cheered.

I smiled and started to take a bow when I noticed a candle still smoldering. I put my hands on my knees and leaned in for a closer look. What was that? I watched in amazement as a flame sprouted from the thin trail of smoke. Then another flame appeared. Then another, until all seven candles were ablaze.

"What?!" I said. "I just blew you out!"

Laughter swept through the crowd and Mommy and Daddy smiled.

"You'll just have to blow them out again," Daddy said.

My stomach felt sick. I didn't know how this

unfortunate event would affect my wish. I had worked so hard and now it was slipping away.

I took another huge breath and blew them out again.

"There," I said. "Now you're out."

Again the candles flickered back to a flame. This couldn't be happening.

"Trick candles?!" I said. "No fair!"

I snatched them off the cake and threw them on the ground. I crushed each one with the heel of my foot, leaving a wax smear on the deck.

"Let's see you come back from that!" I said, smiling.

Everyone roared with laughter.

"Cut the cake already," Cody said.

"I want that piece," Jo-Jo shouted.

"Can I have an ear?" Herby asked.

"An eye for me," Jacob said. "May I please have an eye?"

Mommy portioned out the cake to the hungry mob and Daddy scooped the ice cream. We moved inside with our full plates and sat in a circle around the pile of presents.

"Okay, everyone," Mommy said. "It's present time!"

I tore through the first gift's wrapping paper as everyone watched.

"Hmm," I said, clutching the box. "How can it breathe in there?"

I ripped off the paper and found a box of building blocks.

"Oh," I said. "I like blocks and love to build stuff. Thanks."

I grabbed the next present – it was an envelope.

"Too small," I said and ripped it open. "A gift card! Sweet."

The crowd crept closer with each gift I unwrapped. Fingers, sticky with ice cream and cake, reached for their chance to rip a piece of wrapping paper. There's something about presents that everyone loves. Before I knew it everyone started tearing edges of the gifts I picked up. The flurry of paper ripping left a pile of unwrapped gifts in the center of the floor. There were blocks, gift cards, puzzles, action figures, and stuffed animals, but no Chihuahua.

"Happy Birthday, Max!" everyone shouted. I stood before the pile of shredded paper and gifts.

"Thank you," I said, forcing a smile.

I was thankful and appreciated all the gifts, but

I didn't get the one thing I truly wanted and had wished so hard for.

I sat back down and sank deep into the couch to finish my ice cream and cake.

"What's the matter, Max?" Jo-Jo asked.

"I just don't understand," I said softly. "I tried so hard this year and that's all I've really ever wanted."

"It had to be those trick candles," he said. "I

don't know how to score that one. It might have counted against you."

"Yeah," I said. "I guess there's always next year."

Bing-Bong! Bing-Bong!

My heart raced as the sound of the doorbell pierced the room.

I caught Mommy's gaze and my heart fluttered. She smiled warmly.

"I wonder who that could be," she said.

I dropped my plate and sprinted for the door.

CHAPTER 9

Really and Truly Over

I COULD HARDLY believe it. My heart pumped and pumped as I ran for the door.

Bing-bong! Bing-bong!

"My wish," I said under my breath. "It has to be my wish!"

Jo-Jo sprang up and joined me.

I flung the door open with such force it slammed into the wall with a thud. I didn't have time to care; I had to see what was on the other side.

My face crumbled as the figure at the door became clear. Jo-Jo's face dropped even further and we stood, mouths open.

"Happy Birthday, Max," Jo-Jo's Mom said.

"Oh," I said. "Hello, Jo-Jo's Mom. And thank you."

Jo-Jo ran back into the house, away from his mom.

"Wow," she said. "You guys sure know how to make a lady feel wanted."

I smiled.

"Hello, Mary," Mommy called from behind me. "Come on in, we're just wrapping up."

She chatted with Mommy about the party while Jo-Jo and I gathered his things.

"Thanks for coming over," I said. "I had a great time."

"Me too," he said. "This was the best party ever! I can't wait until next year."

"What was your favorite part?

"Definitely the water balloon fight," he said. "It was epic."

"You're right about that," I said.

"I'm sorry you didn't get your wish. Maybe next year."

"I guess so," I said. "It was still a pretty great day. It just wasn't in the cards apparently."

"See you later, Max."

And with that, Jo-Jo was gone.

The doorbell continued to ring throughout the afternoon. Each time, another friend left until all that remained was wrapping paper, dirty plates, and a few pieces of piñata candy that nobody wanted.

"All right, everyone," Mommy said. "Time to clean up."

"But it's my birthday," I said. "I don't have to, right?"

"Sorry," Mommy said. "It goes along with hosting a party. Please start with the backyard."

"Come on," Cody said. "Wasn't the party worth it?"

"Yes, but I didn't get what I wished for," I said.

"I know you really wanted a Chihuahua," Mommy said. "But that's a big responsibility."

"It's the only thing I've wished for since I can remember," I said. "Every birthday and Christmas, it's the same wish."

We made our way to the backyard to pick up any trash that had missed the can.

"You can't win them all," Cody said.

"Hey, at least you got some pretty cool stuff." he said.

"I sure did."

"What was your favorite?" he asked.

"Probably the robot Chihuahua," I answered. "That's the closest thing to a real dog."

"Cool," he said. "By the way, what did you get from Mommy and Daddy?"

I sat puzzled for a minute, but couldn't put my finger on it.

"I have no idea," I said as a sparkle returned to my eye. "Let's go find out."

We dashed back to the house.

"We finished the trash," Cody said.

Mommy, Daddy, Hunny-G, and G-Dude were all sitting at the kitchen table relaxing.

"Mommy! Daddy!" I said. "What'd you get me for my birthday?"

Daddy looked blankly at me and Mommy smiled.

"What do you mean, Max?" Mommy said.

"My birthday present," I said. "Where is it?"

Mommy chuckled. "What do you think this birthday party was? I heard you say it was the best party ever."

"What?!" I screamed. "The party was my present?!"

"Yes, son," Daddy said, frowning. "The party."

My heart sunk. This was the first time I realized that it was truly over. My wish had not come true.

"Now," Mommy said. "I have one more thing I need you to do."

I couldn't speak, so I just looked up at her as my eyes began to fill with tears.

"Empty the waste-paper baskets in the

bathrooms," Mommy said. "They're always full after a party."

All the happiness drained right out of me. I was so beaten I couldn't even complain.

"I got this one," Cody said and headed for the hallway bathroom.

"Max, you can go empty my bathroom," Daddy said.

I slumped down the hall to their room. I opened the door and felt a cool rush of air as I walked in. The blinds were closed and it was dark. I thought it would make a nice place to cry later. I headed for the bathroom door, which was also closed.

That's funny, I thought. It's usually open. My eyes began to fill with tears as I reached for the door-knob.

When I opened the door, I couldn't believe my eyes. I rubbed them and burst into tears.

Sitting before me, curled up in a ball, was a little white Chihuahua puppy. It was fast asleep on a pillow laid on the bathroom floor.

Tears rolled down my cheeks. I scooped up the sleepy puppy. Its perfect tiny paws stretched as it yawned. She licked the salty tears from my cheeks with her little pink tongue.

I turned to leave the bathroom and saw everyone peering through the doorway with huge smiles on their faces.

"Happy Birthday, Max," they cheered.

I stood speechless, holding my birthday wish. All I could manage was a single sentence whispered in my puppy's ear: "I think I'll name you Birthday Miracle."

From the Author

If you enjoyed this book, please leave an honest review. Word-of-mouth is truly powerful, and your words will make a huge difference. Thank you.

As you read this, I'm writing the next Max E. James adventure. For updates on new releases, promotions, and other great children's book recommendations, join my Kids' Club at:

http://www.maxejames.com/kids-club/

DON'T FORGET YOUR FIRST FREE DOWNLOAD

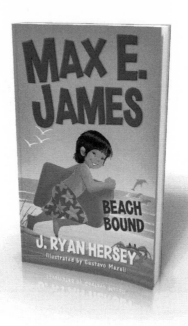

In case you missed it, be sure to pick it up for free!
http://www.maxejames.com/books/beach-bound/

DON'T FORGET YOUR SECOND FREE DOWNLOAD

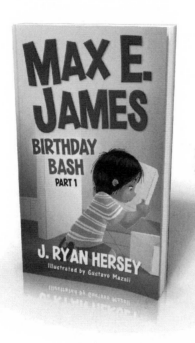

Type the link below into your browser to get started.

http://eepurl.com/cfcfkj

About the Author

J. Ryan Hersey is a devoted father and husband who lives in beautiful Hampton Roads, Virginia. His stories are inspired by the adventures he shares with his wife and two boys. He is author of the Max E. James children's series. To find out more or connect with him directly, visit his website at:

http://www.maxejames.com

About the Illustrator

Gustavo Mazali lives with his family in beautiful Buenos Aires, Argentina. Having drawn all his life, Gustavo has developed the unique ability to capture the essence of children in his art. You can view his portfolio at:

http://www.mazali.com

About the Editor

Amy Betz founded Tiny Tales Editing after working as a children's book editor at several major publishing houses. She lives with her family in Bethel, Connecticut. You can learn more about Amy at:
http://www.tinytalesediting.com

ALL TITLES

Beach Bound
Birthday Bash Part 1
Birthday Bash Part 2
Fishing Fever
Winter Wipeout
Crash Course

Made in the USA
Middletown, DE
24 July 2021